THIS BOOK BELONGS TO:

BARNACLES · INKLING · KWAZII · PESO · BARNACLES · I

TWEAK · DASHI · SHELLINGTON · TUNIP · TWEAK · DASHI

BARNACLES · INKLING · PESO · ACLES · I

TWEAK · DASHI · SHELLINGTON · TUNIP · TWEAK · DASHI

BARNACLES · INKLING · KWAZII · PESO · BARNACLES · I

meomi

WOULD LIKE TO DEDICATE THIS BOOK TO
OUR FAMILIES, FRIENDS AND CRITTER COHORTS.

MEOMI is the creative team of Vicki Wong and Michael C. Murphy who live in Vancouver, Canada with their many sasquatch friends. They enjoy writing silly stories, drinking tea, and drawing strange creatures. Meomi's art and animation has been featured in books, toys and projects worldwide.
Visit them at: www.meomi.com

CHECK OUT THE OTHER BOOKS TOO - I HEAR THEY'RE PRETTY GOOD! GRUMBLE!

First published in hardback in the USA by Immedium Inc. in 2006
First published in hardback in Great Britain by HarperCollins Children's Books in 2009
First published in paperback in 2009

10 9 8 7 6

ISBN: 978-0-00-731250-4

HarperCollins Children's Books is a division of HarperCollins Publishers Ltd.

Text and illustrations copyright © MEOMI Design Inc.: Vicki Wong and Michael Murphy 2006

Published by arrangement with Immedium Inc. immedium www.immedium.com

Visit our website at www.harpercollins.co.uk
Printed in Hong Kong

Edited by Don Menn
Design by Meomi and Elaine Chu

Please be kind to sea monsters.

THE OCTONAUTS

& the Only Lonely Monster

· MEOMI ·

HarperCollins *Children's Books*

It was a quiet and peaceful morning under the deep blue ocean when...

Captain Barnacles was exercising.

Dr Shellington was brushing his teeth.

Professor Inkling was reading the newspaper.

Tunip the Vegimal was cooking breakfast.

Dashi Dog was combing her hair.

Peso Penguin was getting dressed.

Kwazii Kitten was taking a bath.

Tweak Bunny was still asleep!

Kwazii poked his head outside
his bedroom and exclaimed,

WHat's going On?

Quick!

"Get to HQ! The Octopod is in danger!"
Captain Barnacles shouted back as he ran by.

"Octonauts!" Professor Inkling called everyone to order. "According to these charts from our super quantum computers, there is a huge probability that we are...

UNDER attack!

"Octonauts to your stations!
We have to defend the Octopod!"
Captain Barnacles swiftly declared.

Kwazii, Peso and Barnacles rushed down
to the dock, while Tweak prepared the
ships for launch.

The Octonauts shot out of the launch bay and came face to face with a giant MONSTER!
It had large, ferocious eyes and many long, tangly legs which were
wrapped tightly around the Octopod, ready to crush the building to bits!

Kwazii Kitten immediately charged forward in his submarine and crashed valiantly into the giant creature's head! To the Octonauts' surprise, the big, leggy creature suddenly burst into tears!

"A crying monster? That's not scary!"
Captain Barnacles observed.
"Let's ask him some questions!"

Peso cautiously came out
of the ship to help bandage
the whimpering monster.

"Sorry! I didn't realise this was your home! I thought it might be someone like me.

It has a big, round head like me.

It has long legs like me.

It even has pretty eyes like me!" the monster sniffled.

"No! No!" Peso exclaimed. "This is the Octopod, and we live here!

Where is your home?"

"I don't know!"
the monster shook his head sadly.

"I woke up one day in a deep, dark cave,

and I was all alone!"

"I started swimming around to look for others like me...

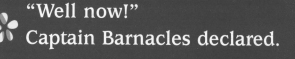

But everyone just wanted to get away from me.

I was so lonely, until I saw your Octopod!"

"Well now!" Captain Barnacles declared.

"This sounds like a job for the Octonauts! I'm sure we can help you."

Kwazii and Peso eagerly agreed because Octonauts always enjoy a good adventure.

The group returned to the Octopod to consult with Professor Inkling.

"Mmm... mmm...
very interesting problem!"
the professor remarked.

"According to the latest
research on the Octo-net
about MOPA-LOPA-TOLOGY
and TENTA-GLYPHICS,
there is a higher occurrence
of colossal cryptozoological
manifestations in polar
magnetic regions."

The Octonauts looked
at Professor Inkling
in confusion.

"Err... try the North Pole!"

The crew packed some supplies and started off on their journey.
"We'll stay here and research. Good luck!" Professor Inkling called after the ship.
Dashi, Tweak and Tunip waved goodbye to their departing Octomates.

First, the Octonauts navigated the North.

Next they searched the South.

Finally, they wandered the West.

He tuwe He?
toKeD YA UN He?
TAHKAA?
SALOON
SASSAFRAS
GENERAL STORE
WANTED
HOWDY

The Octonauts looked EVERYWHERE,
but there were no giant tentacle monsters to be found.

The ship's communicator suddenly called out with a message from Professor Inkling.
"Crew! We've found some important data related to your search.
Please return to the Octopod ASAP or as soon as possible!"

WELCOME HOMF

When the crew arrived home, Professor Inkling,
Dashi and Tweak were waiting outside to greet them.

"Octonauts! I know you've worked very hard
to help our new friend, but unfortunately
the Sea Monster Field Guide reports this creature,
ARCHITEUTHIS COLOSSO NUTOPUS,
is the ONLY one of its kind in the entire ocean!"

Architeuthis
Colosso
Nutopus

Only One

The nutopus cried out.

"I don't want to be the only lonely monster in the world!

I want to be like everyone else!"

Barnacles patted one of the monster's giant tentacles.

"Don't be sad, Architoo...
Archituu...
ARCHIE!"

"Look! I'm the only polar bear who plays the accordion!"

"I'm the only kitten with a hair-ball collection!"

"I'm the only penguin with shiny, white teeth!"

"I'm the only dog who can't dog paddle!"

"I'm the only sea otter
who wears underwear!"

"I'm the only octopus
with disappearing ink!"

"I'm the only bunny
who glows in the dark!"

(...vegimals are all the same!)

Archie gathered up the Octonauts in a big hug.
He's the ONLY monster under the sea with eight new friends!

THE
END

until next time